For Heather and V.G.
K.W.-M.

First published in the United Kingdom in 2000 by
David Bennett Books Limited, United Kingdom.

Text and illustrations copyright © 1999 Ken Wilson-Max.
Style and design of all titles in this series copyright © David Bennett Books.

Ken Wilson-Max asserts his moral right to be identified as the
author and illustrator of this work.

British Library Cataloguing-in-Publication Data:
A catalogue record for this book is available from the British Library.

ISBN 1 85602 375 3

Printed in China.

Max Paints the House

Ken Wilson-Max

DAVID BENNETT BOOKS

It was a beautiful day.
Little Pink woke up before
the others.

Little Pink rushed outside with his paints. "I think I'll surprise everyone," he said.

"I'll paint the house pink to match the pink sky."

So he did. Little Pink stood
back to admire his work.
"I love pink!" he said.

In the house, Max and
Big Blue were having their
favourite breakfast...

… green jelly!
"I've painted the house
to match the sky,"
said Little Pink.
"Come and look."

But now the sky
was turning blue.

"The house doesn't match
the sky," said Big Blue.
"Well it *did*!" said Little Pink.

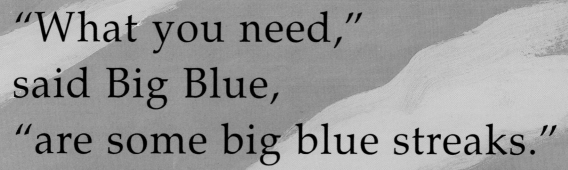

"What you need,"
said Big Blue,
"are some big blue streaks."

"I love blue,"
she said.

Little Pink wasn't happy.
"You've spoiled my
wonderful painting," he said.
"I was only trying
to help," said Big Blue.

The bright yellow
sun shone high
in the sky.

"I'm going to paint a bright
yellow sun," said Max.

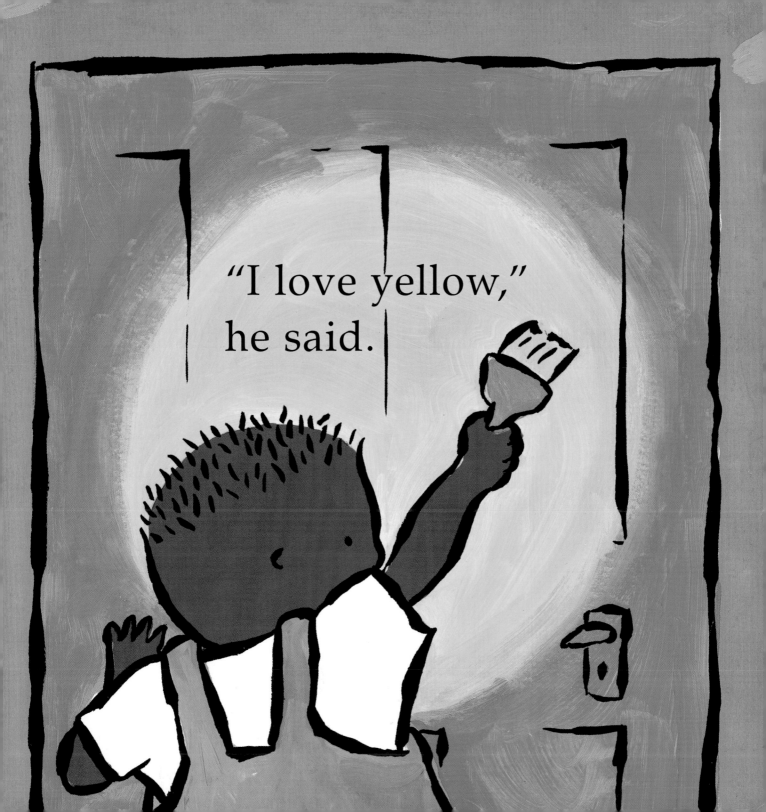

"Now the house really does match the sky," said Max.

But Big Blue wasn't happy.

"You've spoiled *my* painting," she said.

"I was only trying to help," said Max.

"I'm going indoors to have some jelly," said Little Pink.

"So am I,"
said Big Blue.

A big grey cloud appeared
in the sky above the house.
It started to rain.

The rain washed
away all the paint.

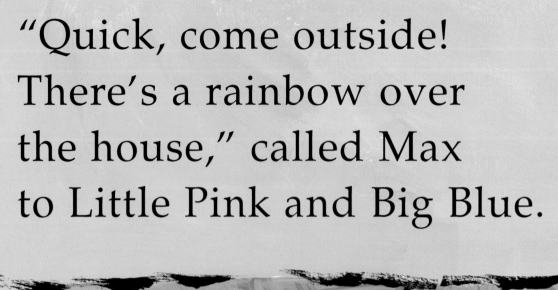

"Quick, come outside!
There's a rainbow over
the house," called Max
to Little Pink and Big Blue.

"Wow! Let's paint the house to match the rainbow," they said. So they did.

"Look! Our rainbow has my favourite colour in it," said Max.
"And mine," said Big Blue.

"It does now," said Max.

Little Pink was very happy.
Big Blue was very happy.
They were all very happy.